Jazz Cats

Jazz Cats

By David Davis

Illustrated by Chuck Galey

PELICAN PUBLISHING COMPANY

Gretna 2004

First printing, September 2001
Second printing, February 2004

To Lynda Moreau, for help along the way.
Also to Nina Kooij, Joseph Billingsley, and Frank McGuire,
for their unsung efforts in dealing with wayward writers.
This book is for you.

The word "Pelican" and the depiction of a pelican are trademarks
of Pelican Publishing Company, Inc., and are registered
in the U.S. Patent and Trademark Office.

Library of Congress Cataloging-in-Publication Data

Davis, David (David R.), 1948-
    Jazz cats / by David Davis.
        p. cm.
    Summary: Cool cats entertain the crowds with their music in the
French Quarter of New Orleans.
    ISBN 1-56554-859-0 (alk. paper)
    [1. Jazz—Fiction. 2. Cats—Fiction. 3. French Quarter (New Orleans,
La.)—Fiction. 4. New Orleans (La.)—Fiction. 5. Stories in rhyme.] I.
Title.
    PZ8.3.D28942 Jaz 2001
    [E]—dc21
                                                                00-050203

Printed in China
Published by Pelican Publishing Company, Inc.
1000 Burmaster Street, Gretna, Louisiana 70053

Jazz Cats

Down in New Orleans where the sounds are sweet,
In a back-alley corner off of Bourbon Street,
There's some hipster kitties (they don't chase no
   rats).
They make swinging music—'cause they're Jazz
   Cats!

Jazz Cats!
Swingin' Jazz Cats!

See them congregated by an old brick wall,
Not too far from the Preservation Hall.
The folks down there never throw a shoe,
'Cause the air is filled with sweet jazz and blues.

Jazz Cats!
Swayin' Jazz Cats!

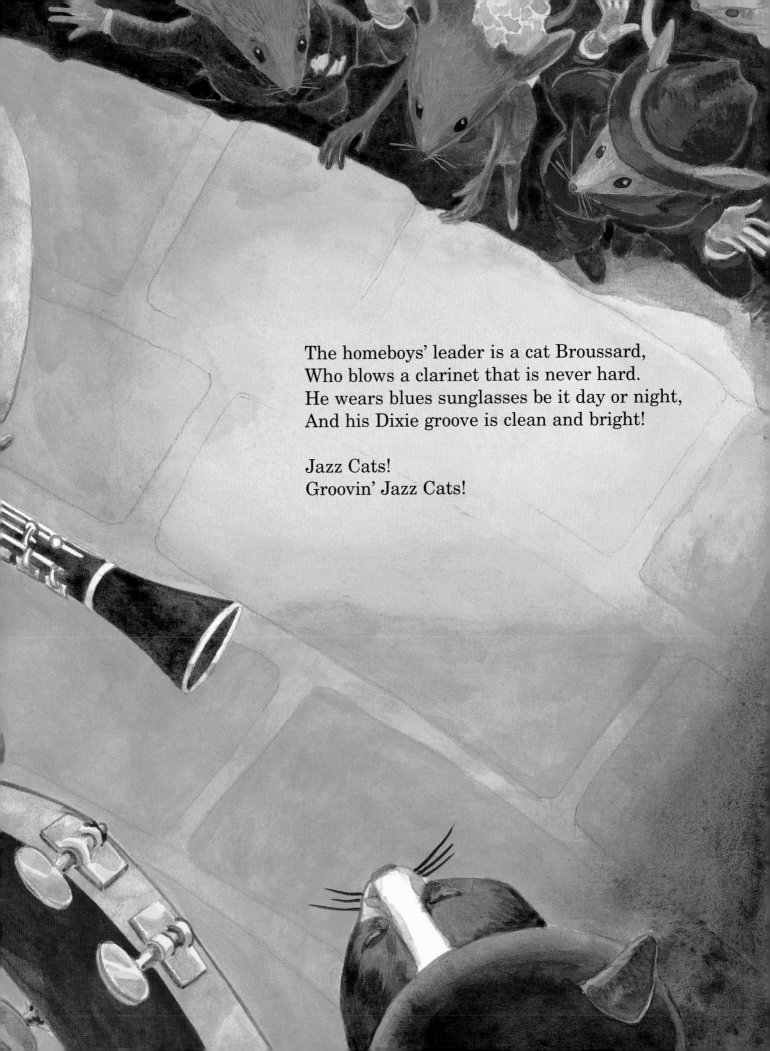

The homeboys' leader is a cat Broussard,
Who blows a clarinet that is never hard.
He wears blues sunglasses be it day or night,
And his Dixie groove is clean and bright!

Jazz Cats!
Groovin' Jazz Cats!

Old Wailing Tijon picks the fiddle bass,
And the beat he plucks is pure Southern grace!
He's a big fat tabby, and his eyes are green,
Got a zoot suit on when he makes the scene!

Jazz Cats!
Wailin' Jazz Cats!

Little skinny Tyrone blows the trumpet sound.
All the windows rattle when he gets unwound!
You can dig him wailing clean to Jackson Square,
And the she-cats gather when he's playing there!

Jazz Cats!
Far-out Jazz Cats!

Old Grandpa Kitty always plays his line.
When his horn starts working, you just blow your mind!
He's a master hepcat on his alto sax,
A real cool daddy from across the tracks!

Jazz Cats!
Real hip Jazz Cats!

They have a hot piano kitty with the name Louise.
She sings along—and she's a cute Siamese.
She plays some Satchmo and some Holiday
Down in the Quarter when these jive cats play.

Jazz Cats!
Singin' Jazz Cats!

Then there's Willard on his trash-can drums,
Pounding out backbeat while the music hums!
He'll play all night for a bowl of milk,
In his derby hat and his shirt of silk!

Jazz Cats!
Rhythm Jazz Cats!

On a summer evening along about nine,
Sneak down the alley—hear those cats unwind!
All the French Quarter kitties go to party there,
And each cat brings along a beau or cher.

Jazz Cats!
Party Jazz Cats!

They don't fear the policeman, 'cause he's so cool;
He stops the traffic to let them through!
The cats go by underneath his hand,
'Cause he wants to hear this back-street band!

Jazz Cats!
Chilled-out Jazz Cats!

They've got crawfish pie and some gumbo too,
And all those kitties wear out their shoes,
Dancing to the music in the bright moonlight.
Man, that kit-cat party is out of sight!

Jazz Cats!
Dancin' Jazz Cats!

They hit those high notes, and they hit those low,
And they don't charge you if you stay or go!
If you dig it, you can request a tune,
'Neath the Southern stars and bright Cajun moon.

Jazz Cats!
Dixie Jazz Cats!

The band keeps jumping 'til the party's through,
Then they get some coffee and a beignet or two,
At their own special table at Café Du Monde,
And they play some more out on the lawn.

Jazz Cats!
Happy Jazz Cats!

When the sun peeps up over Jackson Square
You can see those cats while they're sleepin' there!
Folks hear them purring in the morning light,
Have to get their rest before the gig tonight!

Jazz Cats!
Sleepy Jazz Cats!

A kind market worker slips them a fish,
And a bowl of milk in a china dish,
'Cause everyone hip knows just where it's at.
Those Big Easy folks love these real gone cats!

Jazz Cats!
Swingin' Jazz Cats!

So, come on down to the Crescent City,
Where the nights are magic and the lights are pretty.
Hear those Southern kitties—man, I heard that!
Dig the Dixie jazz of these real cool cats!

Jazz Cats!
Southern Jazz Cats!

Jazz Cats . . .
Swingin' Jazz Cats.
They'll see you, daddy, on the up side. . . .